DRAGON MASTERS

LEGEND OF THE STAR DRAGON

WRITTEN BY

TRACEY WEST

ILLUSTRATED BY

GRAHAM HOWELLS

BRANCHES

SCHOLASTIC INC.

DRAGON MASTERS
Read All the Adventures

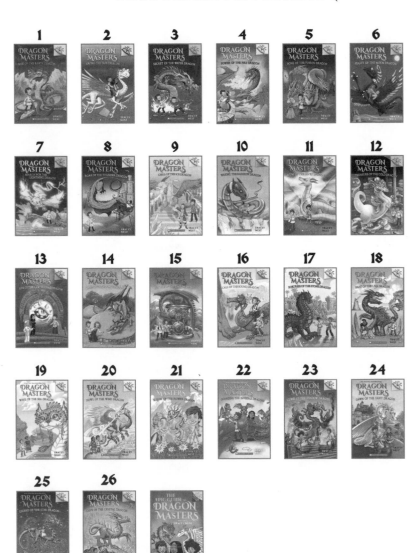

More books coming soon!

TABLE OF CONTENTS

FOR EVANGELINE GOFF,

the inspiration for Stella and a girl who
shines with bright light from within. — TW

While Dragon Masters takes place in a fantasy world, many of the places
and people resemble those here on Earth. The author would like to thank
Vasudha Narayanan, Distinguished Professor of Religion and Director,
Center for the Study of Hindu Traditions (CHiTra) at the University of
Florida, for providing her expertise in the art and history of the Hindu
people for this book.

Text copyright © 2023 by Tracey West
Illustrations copyright © 2023 by Scholastic Inc.
"The Song of the Star Dragon" music by Brittany Abad, copyright © 2023 Pure West Productions, Inc.

All rights reserved. Published by Scholastic Inc., *Publishers since 1920.* SCHOLASTIC, BRANCHES,
and associated logos are trademarks and/or registered trademarks of Scholastic Inc.
The publisher does not have any control over and does not assume any responsibility for
author or third-party websites or their content.

No part of this publication may be reproduced, stored in a retrieval system, or transmitted in any form
or by any means, electronic, mechanical, photocopying, recording, or otherwise, without written
permission of the publisher. For information regarding permission, write to Scholastic Inc.,
Attention: Permissions Department, 557 Broadway, New York, NY 10012.

This book is a work of fiction. Names, characters, places, and incidents are either the product of the
author's imagination or are used fictitiously, and any resemblance to actual persons, living or dead,
business establishments, events, or locales is entirely coincidental.

Library of Congress Cataloging-in-Publication Data

Names: West, Tracey, 1965- author. Howells, Graham, illustrator.
Title: Legend of the Star Dragon / by Tracey West ; [illustrated by Graham Howells].
Description: First edition. New York : Scholastic, Inc., 2023. Series: Dragon Masters ; 25
Audience: Ages 6–8. Audience: Grades 1–3.
Summary: One step closer to stopping the Shadow Dragon from blanketing the world with its
sky-shadow, Drake and the rest of the Dragon Masters must learn how to play the Star Flute in order
to summon the Star Dragon.
Identifiers: LCCN 2023003920 (print) ISBN 9781338777000 (paperback)
ISBN 9781338777017 (library binding)
Subjects: CYAC: Dragons—Fiction. Wizards—Fiction. Magic—Fiction. Flute—Fiction. Adventure and
adventurers—Fiction. BISAC: JUVENILE FICTION / Readers / Chapter Books JUVENILE FICTION /
Action & Adventure / General LCGFT: Action and adventure fiction. Novels.
Classification: LCC PZ7.W51937 Le 2023 (print)
DDC [Fic]—dc23
LC record available at https://lccn.loc.gov/2023003920

10 9 8 7 6 5 4 3 2 1   23 24 25 26 27

Printed in China   62

First edition, December 2023

Illustrated by Graham Howells
Edited by Katie Carella
Book Design by Sarah Dvojack

THE STAR FLUTE

how us the Star Flute, Drake!" Bo urged.

Drake held out the shiny silver flute. Bo and Jean, Dragon Masters just like Drake, leaned in to get a closer look. Behind them, Griffith the wizard nodded thoughtfully.

"That is a very magical object indeed. The magic coming off it is giving me goose bumps!" Griffith said, stroking his beard. "You and Darma did a wonderful job retrieving it, Drake."

The Dragon Masters had been very busy trying to save the world from a dangerous shadow. The sky-shadow blocked all sunlight. Crops were

starting to die. People were cold and scared.

A Dragon Master named Aruna had fed an evil Balam seed to her Shadow Dragon. She had stopped her wizard from eating the seed and she thought it would not affect her dragon. But the seed cursed Chaya, giving the dragon evil powers.

Chaya began absorbing magic being used by wizards around the world. This made Chaya's own powers stronger. It also gave him new powers—like the ability to create the sky-shadow. And because Aruna and Chaya shared a connection, the seed's powers changed her, too.

The Dragon Masters had learned that a Star Dragon could stop the Shadow Dragon. So Drake and Darma went in search of a Light Dragon that could lead them to a Star Dragon.

Dragon Master Rune and his Light Dragon, Lysa, had helped Drake and Darma find the Star Flute. With it, they could finally summon a Star Dragon.

Dragon Masters Rori and Ana had been busy, too. They had warned wizards to stop using magic. Now Chaya was no longer gaining power.

But the Dragon Masters still needed the help of a Star Dragon to get rid of the sky-shadow—and to cure Chaya from the seed's evil magic.

Now home in Bracken Castle, Drake was eager to hear what Bo and Jean had learned while he was away.

"Did you find out how the Star Flute works?" Drake asked.

"No. But we have learned something very important," Jean said. "Star Dragons are born in Helas before they go live in the sky."

"Petra is from Helas!" Drake said. Petra was a Dragon Master, too.

Bo nodded. "We sent Petra a message, asking that she meet you at the library there."

"Petra and her parents should be able to help you learn more about Star Dragons and how to use the flute to summon one," Jean added.

"You and Worm must leave right away, Drake," Griffith said. "Chaya's sky-shadow is already covering the whole world!"

THE GREAT LIBRARY

"haya is one of the most powerful beings in the world right now," Griffith explained. "We must stop this dragon before he uses his new strength to do more harm!"

Drake gently patted his Earth Dragon, Worm. "We haven't slept in a while. Is it okay if we go on our next mission now?"

The green Dragon Stone around Drake's neck glowed as he heard Worm's voice in his head.

Yes, Drake. We must find strength. We are running out of time to stop Chaya.

Drake touched Worm's neck. "Then transport us to the library in Helas!"

Drake's friends waved as Drake and Worm transported in a flash of green light.

Drake blinked. Here, as in Bracken, the dark gray sky-shadow blocked the morning sun. But a huge, ancient building made of white marble cut through the gloom. Tall columns supported the library's two stories. Wide steps led to the great library of Helas.

A girl with curly blond hair ran to greet them. "Drake! Worm!" she cried. A green four-headed dragon followed her out.

"Petra!" Drake gave her a hug.

Worm approached Zera, the Poison Dragon, and lowered his head in greeting. Zera smiled at him with all four of her heads.

"Thanks for meeting us here, Petra," Drake said.

"Bo and Jean told me that there is a way to stop this terrible shadow," Petra said. "I'm happy to help. Come on in! My parents and I have found something."

Drake followed Petra into the library. He gasped. The building was massive! Bookshelves as tall as trees filled the space, every inch holding a book or scroll. Drake spotted a gray kitten playing with a ball of yarn under one of the shelves.

"Is that your cat, the one you named Zera after?" he asked.

Petra grinned. "Yes. Luckily, both Zeras became good friends."

A woman with hair like Petra's and a tall, thin man approached them.

"Mom and Dad, this is Drake," Petra said.

"It is nice to meet you, Drake," said the man. "I am Zale."

"And I am Daria," said Petra's mom. "I wish we could give you a tour of the library, but Bo and Jean wrote us about your mission of great importance. You seek information about Star Dragons."

"Yes," Drake said.

Daria nodded. "We have just the book. Enzo is fetching it now."

She pointed up to the top of a nearby shelf.

A boy, not much younger than Drake and Petra, stood at the top of a ladder.

Enzo grabbed a book and then scrambled down.

"Here you go," the boy said, handing the book to Drake. He had dark blond hair and hazel eyes.

"Thank you," Drake said. "I think I would be nervous to climb all the way up that ladder."

"Enzo is an expert climber, and a great reader, too," Petra said. "He is a big help here at the library."

Enzo grinned. "Thanks, Petra! I really love being around all of the books."

Petra took Drake's hand. "Let's see what we can find out!"

A STARRY TALE

rake and Petra sat down to look at the book together. The title read, *Legend of the Star Dragons*.

Petra opened the book, which was filled with beautiful pictures. She read aloud the tale of the Star Dragons ...

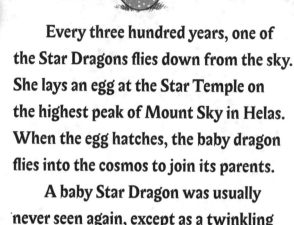

Every three hundred years, one of the Star Dragons flies down from the sky. She lays an egg at the Star Temple on the highest peak of Mount Sky in Helas. When the egg hatches, the baby dragon flies into the cosmos to join its parents.

A baby Star Dragon was usually never seen again, except as a twinkling star in the night sky. Then long ago, a baby Star Dragon named Nova fell to Earth after bumping into an asteroid. Nova was injured, and a girl named Stella helped her heal. When Nova got better, she flew back to the stars.

But Stella missed her dragon friend. So she asked Harmonia, the Goddess of Music, for help. The goddess created the Star Flute.

First, Harmonia played a song to summon Nova back down to the temple. Then she gave Stella a Dragon Stone and Stella became Nova's Dragon Master.

Harmonia played a second song that allowed Stella to stay with Nova in the stars forever.

GODDESS OF MUSIC

"When Stella and Nova flew into the stars, Harmonia hid the flute in a faraway land," Petra read. "But if the flute is found, it may be used to summon Stella and Nova to the temple. They can visit for only a short time, and cannot leave the mountaintop."

Petra turned the page and pointed. "This is the tune to play on the flute! It is beautiful."

"You can read music notes?" Drake asked. "I never learned how to do that."

Petra nodded. "I learned so that I can play the flute when Zera sings."

"Then you should be the one to summon the Star Dragon," Drake said.

"Me?" Petra asked, wide-eyed.

"Yes," Drake replied. "There's only one problem. The Star Dragon won't be able to leave Mount Sky." He took a deep breath. "We will have to lure the Shadow Dragon to the temple!"

CHAPTER 4

HELP FROM DARPAN

ou want to bring the Shadow Dragon *here*, to Helas?" Petra asked with a shiver.

"Yes. This Star Dragon is our only hope of stopping the Shadow Dragon from doing more harm," Drake replied. "We have to bring the two dragons together somehow."

Drake handed Petra the
Star Flute. "Keep this
safe. Worm and I
need to go to Sindhu,
where Chaya and
his Dragon Master,
Aruna, live. Aruna's
brother, Darpan,
may be able to help
us bring the Shadow
Dragon to Mount
Sky. We will meet
you there."

Petra nodded. "I will fly there on Zera. Good
luck, Drake!"

Drake said good-bye and left the library.
Then he touched Worm, and they quickly
transported to Sindhu.

Worm had brought them to a house at the
end of a road, with a moon carved into the front
door. Drake knocked.

A boy with dark brown hair and glasses opened the door. He looked around worriedly.

"Drake! Worm!" Darpan cried. "Why did you come back? If my sister learns you are here, you will be in danger."

"Thank you for helping Jean and me to escape before," Drake said, stepping inside. "I was worried that Chaya might have hurt you after we left."

"Even under the powers of that cursed seed, Aruna knows that I am her brother," Darpan replied. "She will not let her dragon hurt me. But I cannot say the same for you and Worm. Now tell me, why are you here?"

Drake explained that they had found a way to summon the Star Dragon—but only to Mount Sky.

"I need your help. Can you get Aruna and Chaya to Helas?" Drake asked. "Maybe you can tell your sister that wizards are meeting on Mount Sky to try to stop Chaya."

Darpan nodded. "That could work. Chaya might get angry and fly there to stop them."

"Exactly!" Drake said. "It should take some time for Chaya to fly there. In the meantime, Petra and I will summon the Star Dragon."

"I do not like lying to Aruna, but I will do it," Darpan said. "Just promise me that my sister and Chaya will not get hurt."

"We will do everything we can to protect them," Drake promised. "We will save Aruna and Chaya from the Balam seed."

Drake joined Worm outside. "Let's get to Mount Sky," he said. As he closed his eyes, he made a silent wish: *I hope this plan works!*

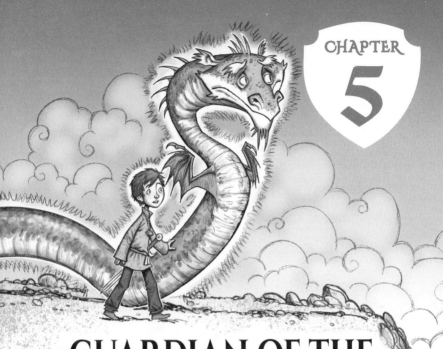

GUARDIAN OF THE TEMPLE

Moments later, Drake and Worm arrived at
Mount Sky. They had landed on a flat area just
below the highest peak of the mountain.

Drake felt a strange crackling of energy in the
air. *It must be because we're so close to the sky-
shadow. We're really high up*, he thought.

23

Petra and Zera stepped out of the gloom. Petra had brought the Star Flute and the book about Star Dragons.

"How did it go in Sindhu?" Petra asked.

"Good! Aruna's brother will help us. I just hope the plan works. If it does, the Shadow Dragon should arrive soon," Drake said. "We need to head to the temple now and summon the Star Dragon."

Petra motioned behind her. "This path will lead us there. But the book says a dangerous creature called a griffin guards the temple."

Drake's Dragon Stone glowed green. He heard Worm's voice in his head.

Petra is right. A dangerous creature awaits us.

"We'll have to get past the creature," Drake said. "The temple is the only place we can summon the Star Dragon."

Petra took a deep breath. "The book tells of one way to deal with the griffin," she said. "Zera and I will have to do it."

"Worm and I will follow your lead, then," Drake said.

Petra and Zera started up the path. Drake and Worm followed.

The four of them soon reached the top of the mountain. Ahead stood a white marble temple. Star-shaped symbols were carved across the beam on top of the columns.

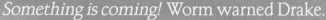

Something is coming! Worm warned Drake.

A creature stepped onto the path, blocking their way. The beast had the body of a lion, and the head and wings of an eagle.

"Begone from here!" the griffin screeched.

"We're on an important mission," Petra said. "Please let us pass."

"Begone!" the griffin screeched again. "Or face my wrath, the wrath of the guardian of the Star Temple. Beware my claws!"

Petra's Dragon Stone glowed. Petra leaned in to Zera and whispered, "Sing the griffin's lullaby!"

The Poison Dragon's four heads began to sing.

A SURPRISE IN THE SHADOWS

era sang a calming, peaceful tune. The guardian yawned and its eyes began to droop. It struggled to stay awake.

"Begone. . ." The griffin began but trailed off. ". . . zzzzzzzzzzz."

Petra put a finger to her lips and Zera stopped singing. Then she motioned for Drake and Worm to follow her. They tiptoed past the sleeping beast and continued toward the marble temple.

"That was incredible," Drake said, looking over his shoulder.

Petra patted the book. "I read more while you were in Sindhu. That song will keep the griffin asleep for a day and a night."

"We are lucky to have a singing dragon with us!" Drake said. He looked up at the sky-shadow. "We should summon the Star Dragon now. We will need time to explain everything to Stella and Nova before Aruna and Chaya get here."

Petra handed the book to Drake. "Can you please hold this open for me while I play the notes?"

Drake opened it to "The Song of the Star Dragon." Petra raised the Star Flute to her lips and began to play.

"Oops!" said Petra. "My hands are shaking a little and I played a wrong note. Let me start over."

Suddenly, a dark, swirling portal appeared overhead in the sky-shadow.

Drake looked up hopefully. *Is the song working before Petra has even finished?*

A dragon flew out of the portal—a dragon with gray feathered wings, long white tusks, and glowing red eyes. His Dragon Master had gray hair, and her eyes glowed red, too.

Drake gasped. "Chaya and Aruna! They got here faster than I thought they could!"

Petra stopped playing the flute and stared at the Shadow Dragon.

Then Drake noticed something—Darpan was hanging from Chaya's tail!

Chaya landed on top of the marble temple. Darpan jumped down and ran over to Drake.

"I'm sorry!" Darpan said. "I didn't know that Chaya could create portals to travel through the sky-shadow. There was no way to warn  you we'd arrive so soon!"

Worm and Zera faced Chaya, ready to spring into action.

Aruna glared at her brother.

"Darpan!" she snapped. "Why are Drake and these dragons here? Where are the wizards you told us about?"

Darpan stammered. "I—I . . ."

Drake stepped forward. "Darpan just wants to help you," he said. "We can summon a Star Dragon to this temple. If you could listen—"

Chaya flew down to the temple steps and roared.

RAWWWWWWWWWWWWR!

The powerful, angry roar knocked Drake, Petra, and Darpan off their feet. The Star Flute fell out of Petra's hands.

Drake grabbed the flute as it rolled off the edge of the peak.

Aruna climbed off Chaya's back. She glared at Drake, Petra, and Darpan.

"Chaya, destroy the Star Temple now!" she commanded.

BREAKING THROUGH

Drake thought quickly. *If Chaya destroys the temple, we might never be able to summon the Star Dragon!*

"Worm, stop Chaya!" Drake yelled.

"Zera! Use your stun poison!" Petra cried.

Worm's body glowed green. Zera's body did, too.

Worm shot a beam of light at Chaya. The Shadow Dragon ducked.

Then Zera's four heads sprayed shimmering yellow droplets all over Chaya.

The Shadow Dragon froze in place.

"Wow!" Drake cried. "Petra, what did Zera just do?"

"We have been experimenting with different poisons Zera can create," Petra replied. "This one makes anything it touches stop moving. But it only lasts for a little while."

Aruna stomped toward them. "Fools! Don't you realize how very powerful Chaya is? Your dragons' weak powers will not hold him for long!"

Darpan ran to his sister. "Aruna, please," he pleaded. "Listen to these Dragon Masters. They know a way to help you both."

"We do not need help!" Aruna snapped. She raised her arms toward the sky. "Can't you see how beautiful this shadow is? Chaya and I are so powerful. We can do anything we want!"

"The Aruna *I* know wants to help everyone," Darpan told her. "Stop the sky-shadow, and you will help the world."

Aruna's eyes flickered. She paused. "I will never destroy Chaya's sky-shadow!"

Darpan turned to Drake and Petra, shaking his head. "It's no use. I cannot get through to her."

An idea popped into Drake's mind. His Dragon Stone glowed. "Worm, can you use your powers to help Darpan get through to his sister?"

I think so, Worm replied. *It is the Balam seed inside Chaya that is making Aruna evil, too. With Chaya frozen, there is a chance I can use my powers to break their connection for a few moments. Then Aruna will lose her connection to the seed.*

Drake nodded. "Darpan, talk to Aruna. Worm will help you get through to her."

Soft green light shone from Worm's eyes onto Aruna.

Darpan looked at his sister. "Please, Aruna. What good is Chaya's power if plants will die and people will starve? I know you don't want that."

As Darpan spoke, his sister's eyes flickered again.

"I—I don't know . . . ," she stammered.

"Aruna, listen to me!" Darpan pleaded. "None of this is your fault. You are not evil. Neither is Chaya. This all started when you fed Chaya the Balam seed. We know you meant well. And we can help you fix things—if you'll let us."

Aruna shook her head. "But . . . Chaya . . ."

"Chaya knows how much you love him, just as I love you," Darpan said. "Let us help you both."

The red glow faded from Aruna's eyes. Her gray hair returned to a glistening black color.

Worm stopped shining his green light on her.

Aruna blinked, then threw her arms around Darpan. "Brother!" she cried. "I am so sorry. I never—"

RAAAAWWWWWWWWR! Chaya roared and stomped.

"Zera's poison has worn off!" Petra shouted.

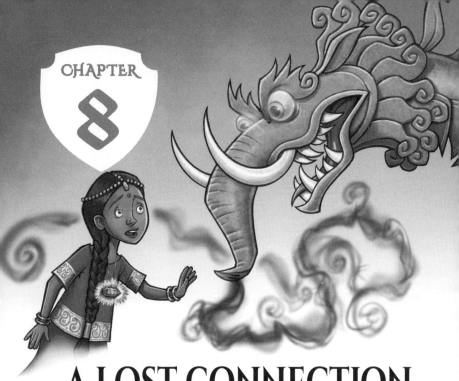

A LOST CONNECTION

Aruna's Dragon Stone glowed as she stepped toward the angry Shadow Dragon.

"Chaya, calm down," she said in a slow, careful voice. "You must not attack Darpan or our new friends. They are here to help us. I made a mistake when I fed you the Balam seed. We must make things right."

RAAAAWWWWWWR! Chaya, his eyes still red from the cursed seed inside him, roared again.

Wisps of gray shadow flowed through Chaya's nose. Like a rope, the shadowy tendril wrapped around the chain of Aruna's Dragon Stone. Then the shadow yanked the stone from her neck!

"Noooooooo!" Aruna cried.

The shadow tendril curled back up toward Chaya. The dragon flew up, and then dropped the Dragon Stone off of the mountain peak!

Oh no! Now Aruna can no longer communicate with Chaya, Drake realized.

The Shadow Dragon roared again, and his whole body began to shine with gray light.

Dozens of creatures flew down from the sky-shadow—creatures made of shadow with glowing eyes and long arms.

"Shadow phantoms!" Drake yelled, warning the others. "Don't let them touch you! Worm, try to slow them down."

Worm's eyes shone green, and glowing green bubbles appeared all around him. The bubbles floated through the air, absorbing any shadow phantoms they came in contact with.

"Great new bubble power, Worm!" Drake cheered.

Then Petra yelled, "Zera, stun Chaya again! And get those phantoms next!"

Zera blasted Chaya with a powerful mist of yellow poison. The Shadow Dragon froze in place.

But the shadow phantoms kept zooming down from the sky.

Zera's four heads shot green poison blasts at four shadow phantoms. When the poison hit, the phantoms dissolved.

"Drake, hand me the flute!" Petra yelled. "We need to summon the Star Dragon now!"

Drake ran toward Petra, holding out the silver flute.

Whoosh! One of the shadow phantoms grabbed it from Drake!

Aruna pulled the flute away from the shadow phantom.

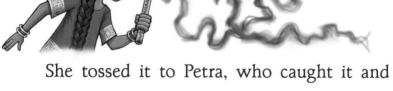

She tossed it to Petra, who caught it and brought it to her lips.

Drake tossed Darpan the *Legend of the Star Dragons* book next. "Petra needs the music!" he cried.

Darpan opened the book to the page of music notes.

Then Petra began to play "The Song of the Star Dragon" once more.

THE SUMMONING

Drake, Aruna, Worm, and Zera fought off the shadow phantoms as Petra played the Star Flute. The enchanted, airy tune echoed across the mountain.

Worm created more green bubbles to absorb the shadow phantoms.

Zera flew overhead. She hit the phantoms with green poison mist to dissolve them.

Aruna threw rocks at them.

And Drake, with both hands now free, took his silver sword from his belt. A shadow phantom floated toward him.

"Ayaaah!" he yelled, thrusting the sword into the shadow phantom.

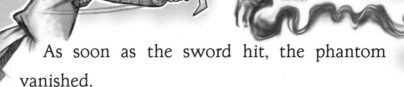

As soon as the sword hit, the phantom vanished.

"Yes!" Drake cheered, but then he heard a cry overhead.

Zera was tumbling out of the sky!

Petra stopped playing the flute. "Zera!" she cried.

"Worm, stop Zera's fall! I'll protect you," Drake yelled. "Petra, keep playing!"

Drake ran to Worm and began slashing any shadow phantoms that came near. Worm's eyes glowed. Green energy surrounded Zera as Worm used his mind powers to gently lower her to the ground.

Drake immediately saw what was wrong. One of Zera's wings was turning into a shadow!

Drake had seen this before, when a shadow phantom had touched Jean in Sindhu. If Shu the Water Dragon hadn't saved her, her whole body would have turned into a shadow. But Shu was not here.

"A shadow phantom touched Zera's wing," Drake explained to the others. "We can't help her on our own. But hopefully, the Star Dragon can help her!"

I hope the Star Dragon can save us all! thought Drake.

Petra finished the song and ran to Zera's side.

Suddenly, a circle of glittering light broke through the sky-shadow. Startled, the shadow phantoms scattered, disappearing back into the gloom.

A dragon swooped down from the sky.

"Nova!" Drake cheered.

STELLA AND NOVA

Everyone stared at the beautiful sight as the Star Dragon hovered above Mount Sky. Dark blue scales rippled down Nova's long, curved body, and each scale shimmered with starlight.

We are lucky, Worm told Drake. *This is a dragon very few have seen.*

A girl with long, pale blue hair rode on Nova's back. Purple eyes sparkled in her round, friendly face. A white Dragon Stone shone around her neck.

"Hello," Stella said, in a light, musical voice. "It has been a long time since Nova and I have been summoned. Does this have something to do with the strange shadow that covers the sky?"

Aruna stepped forward. "Yes, Stella. I fed my Shadow Dragon, Chaya, a Balam seed. I hoped I could save my wizard Vanad from turning evil."

"You *did* save your wizard, Aruna," Drake interrupted her.

"Yes, what you did was very brave, sister," Darpan added.

Aruna frowned. "I thought I could save the world. But I made a mistake. In the process, Chaya became evil. And now the world is in danger."

Stella's eyes turned to the Shadow Dragon, still frozen on top of the marble temple.

"I understand," Stella said. "Nova's light is indeed powerful enough to cast the Balam seed out of your dragon. But why is Chaya not moving? Is he under some kind of spell?"

"My dragon, Zera, froze Chaya with a poison stun attack," Petra replied. "But the poison will wear off soon, and now Zera is hurt."

Stella nodded. "I know what to do." She closed her eyes, and her white Dragon Stone glowed brightly.

"Please do not hurt Chaya," Aruna pleaded. "This is not his fault."

"Nova's powers will not harm him," Stella promised. "Ready, Nova?"

The Star Dragon nodded her graceful neck and flew toward Chaya...

THE SKY BATTLE

As the Star Dragon approached Chaya, the Shadow Dragon's eyes blinked.

"Nova, Star Beams!" Stella commanded.

Beams of bright white starlight shone from Nova's eyes, aimed at Chaya. But the poison wore off! The Shadow Dragon roared and flew off the temple, escaping Nova's beams.

Petra frowned worriedly. "I wish Zera and I could help them."

"Worm, can *we* help?" Drake asked.

Let us watch and see, Worm replied. *Nova is very powerful and Stella knows what to do.*

The Star Dragon and Shadow Dragon flew up toward the gloom of the sky-shadow.

"Nova, Star Dust!" Stella cried.

Nova sang a loud high note, and a cloud of glittering dust appeared. The dust swirled around Chaya.

Chaya roared, and a shadow cloud streamed from his mouth. It absorbed the glitter.

"Nova, Star Beams again!" yelled Stella.

Two more beams of starlight shone from Nova's eyes. Just before they could zap Chaya, the Shadow Dragon disappeared into a portal in the sky-shadow.

Then Chaya reappeared behind Nova.

Aruna watched the battle, biting her lower lip. "I wish I could communicate with Chaya. I need my Dragon Stone!"

Darpan ran to where Chaya had tossed his sister's Dragon Stone. He carefully lay down to peer over the edge of the mountainside. "Aruna, I see it! Your stone is on a ledge down below! I can't reach it!"

"Worm can get it for you," Drake offered. But at that moment, two shadow phantoms zipped toward Aruna.

"Worm, stop them!" Drake commanded.

Worm trapped the shadow phantoms in green bubbles.

Overhead, Stella made another command. "Nova, Star Whip!"

Nova's long, curved tail whipped in the sky, creating a rope of starlight.

The light wrapped around Chaya's body. He shrieked and tried to cast if off.

"Nova, power up!" Stella commanded.

While Chaya struggled to shake free of Nova's bonds of light, Nova closed her eyes. The thousands of tiny stars on her scales began to grow brighter and brighter ...

Raaaaawwwwwwwwwwr!

Chaya burst through his bindings with an explosion of glowing gray shadow beams. Worm glanced over, wanting to help. But three shadow phantoms zipped toward Zera, and Worm shot bubbles at them.

The Shadow Dragon flapped his wings.

"Watch out, Stella! Chaya's going to send you and Nova into the Shadow World!" Aruna cried.

Aruna turned to Drake and Darpan. "I can't let that happen!"

She ran to the edge of the mountain and jumped down!

SUPER SHINE!

Drake and Darpan ran to the edge and looked down. They found Aruna standing on a narrow ledge, holding her Dragon Stone. She knotted the broken end of the chain and put it around her neck.

"Help me pull her up!" Darpan said. He reached for Aruna and she grasped his hand. Drake steadied Darpan as he pulled his sister to safety.

In the sky, Chaya advanced on Stella and Nova, with his wings opened wide. But the Star Dragon wasn't moving out of the way.

"As soon as Chaya wraps his wings around Stella and Nova, they'll be sent to the Shadow World!" Drake cried.

"I'll connect with him," Aruna said, closing her eyes. Then she opened them, frowning. "It's not working. Maybe I need to get closer to him."

"Worm can move you up there with his powers," Drake offered.

Aruna nodded. "Quickly, please!"

Drake turned to Worm. "Send Aruna up to Chaya!"

Worm's eyes glowed green.

Aruna floated up into the air. "Stella, move Nova away from Chaya!" she called out.

Nova's scales shone more brightly.

"I cannot," Stella said. "Nova is charging up for her strongest power, Super Shine. She cannot move or use another power once she starts."

Aruna's Dragon Stone glowed. "Chaya, stop this right now!" she commanded.

Chaya's eyes flashed red.

"Yes, you must listen to me," Aruna told him. "We have a connection. A connection that even the Balam seed cannot break."

Chaya's wings drooped a little.

"Chaya, retreat!" Aruna yelled. "I am your Dragon Master!"

Chaya flew back to the top of the marble temple.

"Thank you, Chaya!" Aruna said. "You did the right thing."

Worm lowered Aruna to the ground.

"Chaya will not stop you!" Aruna called up to Stella. "But the power of the seed inside him is strong. Please help him before it is too late— and before the seed affects me again, too!"

Nova was glowing brightly now—so brightly that everyone had to shield their eyes.

"We are ready," Stella said. "Nova, perform Super Shine!"

CLEAR SKIES

A dazzling burst of white light exploded from every inch of Nova's body.

The light hit Chaya. It lifted the dragon up toward the sky-shadow.

The Shadow Dragon's whole body gleamed with white light. His mouth opened. A tiny seed floated out.

The seed floated higher into the sky, above Chaya and Nova. As it floated, the seed turned into a bright, glowing ball of energy.

Then … *BOOM!*

The seed exploded, sending waves of sparkling white light stretching across the sky! The bright white light extended farther and farther out, continuing to spread all around the world. Every bit of the sky-shadow that it touched dissolved.

"Zera is healed!" Petra cried, hugging her dragon's neck. Zera's wing was solid once more. "The Super Shine must have done it."

Drake gazed up at the sky. "Look!" he cried. "With the shadow gone, you can see the stars."

Chaya floated back down to the ground and lay still, his eyes closed.

"Chaya!" Aruna ran to him.

The shine faded from Nova's body, and she landed in front of the temple.

"The sky-shadow is no more," Stella announced. "And the Shadow World has been destroyed as well."

"Will Chaya be all right?" Aruna asked, tearfully.

Stella nodded. "He will recover. All he needs is time," she replied. "But others around the world might still need help."

Stella opened her left hand. A small glittering white stone magically appeared on her palm. She held it out toward Aruna.

"This is a Star Stone," she said. "It can be used to help anyone who was harmed by Chaya's shadow powers."

Aruna took it from her. "Thank you," she said. "I will make sure to help everyone who needs it."

"I will aid you, sister," Darpan added.

"And now Nova and I must return to the stars," Stella said.

"Thank you, Stella," Drake said. "We will never forget you!"

Stella smiled. "You are all part of my legend now. Good-bye, my friends!"

The Dragon Masters waved as Nova flew up into the night sky.

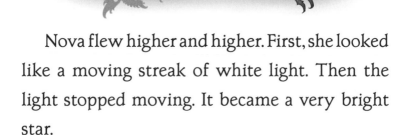

Nova flew higher and higher. First, she looked like a moving streak of white light. Then the light stopped moving. It became a very bright star.

Drake pointed. "Those stars around Nova make the shape of a dragon. And Nova is one of the eyes!" he cried.

WIZARD WORRIES

"In Helas, we call those stars the Draco constellation," Petra explained to Drake, Aruna, and Darpan. "I wonder if that is where all the Star Dragons live."

Aruna stroked Chaya's neck. The dragon's eyes fluttered open. He lifted his head.

"Chaya! You're back!" Aruna cried, hugging him. "Oh, I am so sorry. This is all my fault. You turned evil only because I didn't want Vanad to eat the—"

"Vanad!" Drake remembered. "The last time we saw your wizard, he had turned into a shadow and was stuck in the Shadow World."

Darpan frowned. "Nova destroyed the Shadow World. I hope Vanad was not destroyed, too."

"Brother, we must return to Sindhu at once and try to find him," Aruna said.

"Worm can take you there," Drake offered. "We'd like to help."

Aruna turned to Petra. "Before we go, I must thank you and your dragon. I do not even know your names!"

Petra grinned. "I'm Petra, and my dragon is Zera," she said. "We were happy to help. That's what Dragon Masters do."

Petra gave the Star Flute to Drake and climbed onto Zera's back. "Good-bye, Drake! You know where to find me if you need me."

"Thanks, Petra. I'll miss you," Drake said.

Then Zera flew back to the great library.

"Aruna and Darpan, touch Worm. Then, Aruna, touch Chaya," Drake explained. "Once we're all connected, Worm can transport us."

Aruna and Darpan obeyed.

"Worm, take us to Sindhu!" Drake cried.

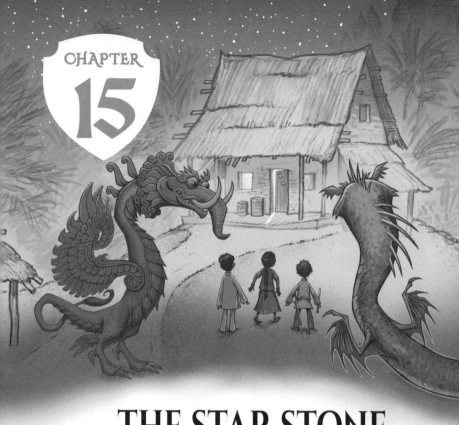

THE STAR STONE

Worm brought Drake, Aruna, Darpan, and Chaya outside Vanad's house. It was nighttime in Sindhu, too. Stars glittered in the night sky. The sleeping residents had no idea yet that the sky-shadow was gone for good.

There was a moon carved into Vanad's front door, which was partly open. Lantern light shone through the windows.

And they could all hear a voice muttering inside: "Let's see. Shadows . . . There must be something useful in one of these scrolls."

Worm and Chaya waited outside while Drake, Aruna, and Darpan rushed in.

"Vanad?" Aruna asked loudly.

"Aruna?"

A shadowy figure floated toward them.

"Aruna! My dear girl, you are your old self!" the wizard cried. "And Darpan, good to see you, my boy. And other boy, I know you somehow..."

"I'm Drake," Drake said. "We met in the Shadow World. I'm so glad we found you!"

Vanad nodded. "Yes, yes, that's right. Strange thing about that Shadow World. One moment I was in it, and the next, I wasn't. But I am still a shadow. So I'm hoping to find answers in my books."

Aruna quickly told him everything that had happened and held out the Star Stone. "Stella said this would help anyone who was harmed by Chaya's shadow powers, but—"

As she spoke, the Star Stone began to glow in her hand. A light shone on Vanad.

When it hit him, he transformed from a shadow back into a solid human.

"Oh my!" he said, touching his arms and legs to make sure it was true. "How wonderful! I'm back! I'm back!"

Suddenly, they heard voices outside.

"The sky-shadow is gone!"

"I see stars!"

Everyone hurried outside. People were now streaming out of their homes and looking up at the sky. First, they stared. Then they cheered. Some began to dance.

"Well, I'm glad everything is back to normal," Drake said. "Now Worm and I should return the Star Flute to—"

"Nonsense, my boy! That can wait," Vanad said. "Now we must celebrate!"

A FRIEND IN NEED

rake and Worm celebrated with their new friends under the night sky. They listened to music and ate delicious food that was spicier than Drake had ever eaten before.

85

Then Drake lay down next to Worm. He slept deeply for the first time since the sky-shadow had appeared. Worm's tail curled around him, and the Earth Dragon snored softly along with Drake.

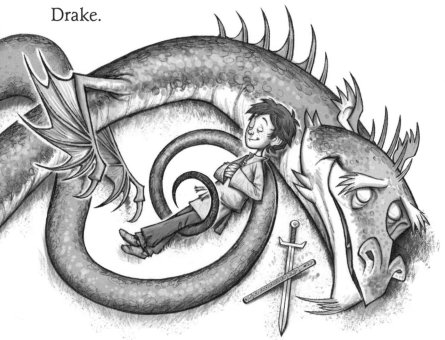

When Drake woke up, Aruna and Darpan were sitting on a blanket next to them. They offered Drake and Worm fruit from a big bowl, and rounds of warm flatbread. They ate until their bellies were full.

"Thank you," Drake said, stretching. He looked up at the sun shining in the blue sky. "Isn't that a beautiful sight?"

"I'll be grateful for every sunrise from now on," Aruna replied.

Drake stood up. "Worm and I need to return the Star Flute to its secret location. And our friends back home will be missing us."

"I understand," Aruna said. She patted her pocket. "Darpan, Chaya, and I will be busy looking for people who need the Star Stone's help. If you find anyone who was hurt by Chaya's shadow powers, please let me know."

"I will. Now that wizards can use magic again, our wizard can send messages to Vanad," Drake said. "Good-bye! I hope we will meet again."

"I hope so, too," Darpan said. "Be well, Drake!"

Drake touched Worm's neck. "Let's return the flute, Worm!"

Seconds later, they landed in front of a shimmering crystal castle. A white dragon and a boy with red hair were outside, staring at the blue sky.

Drake waved at Lysa the Light Dragon and Rune, her Dragon Master. Rune was Deaf, and Drake didn't know enough sign language yet to communicate with him. The boys used their dragons for that.

"Hello"

Drake heard Worm's voice in his head.

*Rune says: You did it, Drake! And I'm glad
you came back right away with the flute. Your
friend Ana flew here yesterday with a message.
I have some news for you. Your wizard, Griffith,
is missing!*

TRACEY WEST got the idea for this book by looking up at the stars and imagining what kinds of dragons might live there. In our world, you can look for a constellation named Draco in the northern sky.

Tracey is the author of the *New York Times* bestselling Dragon Masters series and dozens more books for kids. She shares her home with her husband, her dogs, and a bunch of chickens. They live in the misty mountains of New York State, where it is easy to imagine dragons roaming free in the green hills.

GRAHAM HOWELLS lives with his wife and two sons in west Wales, a place full of castles, and legends of wizards and dragons.

There are many stories about the dragons of Wales. One story tells of a large, legless dragon—sort of like Worm! Graham's home is also near where Merlin the great wizard is said to lie asleep in a crystal cave.

Graham has illustrated several books. He has created artwork for film, television, and board games, too. Graham also writes stories for children. In 2009, he won the Tir Na N'Og award for *Merlin's Magical Creatures*.

DRAGON MASTERS
LEGEND OF THE STAR DRAGON

Questions and Activities

In Chapter Six, Chaya and Aruna surprise everyone by appearing on Mount Sky early. How did they get there so quickly?

Darpan helps Aruna break her connection to the Balam seed. He had tried to get through to her before, but it didn't work. Why does it work this time? Reread page 39.

Do you read music or know someone who does? If so, try playing the tune found on page 16. (Note: You need to be on Mount Sky and use the Star Flute for a Star Dragon to appear.)

The Star Stone can help people harmed by Chaya's shadow powers. Who do you think Aruna and Darpan will help? Write a story about this magic stone!

Have you ever looked for constellations? With an adult, step outside on a clear night and look up at the sky. Use a book or an app to help you identify the constellations you can see.